Love Town

by Michael Kaplan

SAMUELFRENCH.COM

MUSIC USE NOTE

IMPORTANT BILLING AND CREDIT
REQUIREMENTS

LOVE TOWN had its premiere at The Pewter Plough Playhouse in Cambria, California on May 1, 2009. The performance was directed by Karen Moncharsh. The sets were designed by Jim Buckley. The production manager was Kathryn Kenny. The cast was as follows:

KARL . . . . .Gregg Wolff

LYLE . . . . .Craig Brooke

MINDY. . . . . .Karen Moncharsh

GAIL . . . . Sharyn Young

LESTER . . . . .Donn Clarius

RUSSELL. . . . . Daniel Harris

GINA . . . . .MacKenzie Allen

ALEX . . . . Blake Spiller

TOURISTS. . . . . Kathryn Kenny & James Lee Buckley

CUSTOMERS. . . . . Anne Zinke & Colleen Spiller

CHARACTERS

KARL – 40s. The unlikely proprietor of Mary's Cozy Corner. Prone to bouts of bitterness.

LYLE – Early 30s. An upbeat surfer who doesn't do well with responsibility.

MINDY – Early 30s. Ambitious, romantic, wound a little too tight.

GAIL – Late 50s. Karl's landlady. Stylish, controlling, very together.

LESTER – 70s. Wealthy, irritable, easily distracted.

GINA – 17. A goth girl full of teen cynicism.

RUSSELL – 28. A scruffy local.

ALEX – 18. A cool kid without much direction.

MISC. CUSTOMERS AND COUPLES – Tourists mainly in the 20-40 range. They can be double-cast as necessary.

SETTING

The action takes place in Mary's Cozy Corner, a souvenir shop that preys on the tourist trade, located in Sea Spray, California.

TIME

Act One, Scene One: A July morning.
Act One, Scene Two: One week later.
Act Two: November, four months later.
Act Three: April, five months later.

For Frances

ACT ONE

Scene One

(Lights up on Mary's Cozy Corner, a souvenir shop in Sea Spray, California. It is full of curios and knickknacks, the sort that are irresistible to people on vacation. The theme is love and little-town romance by the sea. Fuzzy stuffed seals, shells glued into heart shapes, T-shirts with slogans like **I ♥ Sea Spray**, **Lucky in Love** *and* **Just Engaged**.*)*

(Sitting very still behind the counter is **KARL**. *He is lost in thoughts that do not look happy.)*

(The door opens and a young **MAN** *and* **WOMAN** *enter hand in hand. They make their way through the shop, whispering and ad-libbing reactions ["cuuuute!"] to some of the items they see.)*

(After a moment the **WOMAN** *approaches* **KARL**, *holding up a* **Lucky in Love** *shirt.)*

WOMAN. Do you have this in a medium?

*(**KARL** does not respond.)*

MAN. Excuse me.

KARL. What?

WOMAN. Do you have this in women's medium?

KARL. I don't know.

(The couple exchange a mildly exasperated look.)

WOMAN. Could you look in the back?

KARL. Why?

WOMAN. To see if you have one.

KARL. I wouldn't know where to look.

MAN. You're kidding, right?

KARL. No.

> *(pause)*

WOMAN. I really like this shirt.

KARL. I understand.

WOMAN. Will you please please go look?

KARL. Listen. Isn't it enough that you *feel* Lucky in Love?

MAN. Excuse me?

KARL. Do you really think wearing that shirt will make you *luckier*? Or is this one of those cases where you've got nagging doubts, you just had brunch and you realize he chews all funny.

MAN. Hey!

KARL. But maybe if you plaster your chest with some over-the-top advertisement that you're happy, maybe you'll start to feel happy and the next meal will go better and you'll…what's the thing they say?

WOMAN. Who?

KARL. In 12 step.

WOMAN. Fake it 'til you make it?

KARL. There you go. That would be more honest. A women's medium that says, "I'm Gonna Fake it 'til I Make it."

> *(pause)*

MAN. We just got engaged.

KARL. Everybody gets engaged. This is Sea Spray. We're the magical weekend town.

MAN. So don't sit there and tell us anything about who we are or what we're feeling because I'll ram this hanger down your throat.

> *(Their standoff is interrupted by the phone ringing.)*

KARL. *(answering)* Mary's Cozy Corner. No, Mary's not around. No, I don't.

> *(beat)*

Well, she pretty much disappeared.

(beat)

This is her homicidal husband who got stuck with the store. And I bet you'd love to sell me something adorable. Hello?

(They've obviously hung up. **KARL** *puts down the phone and smiles at his customers.)*

I'm sorry, what were you saying?

(The couple back nervously away from the counter and out the door.)

*(***KARL*** *sighs. He sits there like a caged animal.)*

*(***LYLE*** *and* **MINDY** *enter. She carries a paper plate of baked treats.)*

LYLE. Hey neighbor!

MINDY. I was just saying to Lyle, I didn't know if we were ever going to see this shop open again and wouldn't that be a shame.

LYLE. I'm Lyle. My wife, Mindy.

MINDY. We're just across the street. *Epiphanies.*

KARL. Epiphanies?

MINDY. The most romantic moments of your life. We do sunset proposals, skywriting, moonlight serenades.

LYLE. "From Whims to Weddings."

MINDY. That was mine.

LYLE. "If you can dream it, we can scheme it."

MINDY. Sweetie, we don't use that one. It's got an icky subtext.

(back to **KARL***)*

We just confirmed, we'll be doing tonight, this lovely boy from Anaheim, he's going to walk his girlfriend out by Otter Point and round the rocks at low tide and there in shells and dozens and dozens of peacock feathers it's going to say: Marry Me Ramona. Right on the sand.

(pause)

These are for you. Gluten-free scones.

KARL. That's very kind.

MINDY. Well we need to look out for each other. We were just voted #3 Little Town Main Street in the Western United States.

KARL. What'd we win?

(She almost glares at him…but laughs instead.)

MINDY. You're silly. When those *touristas* are hoofing it up and down, a locked door corner space is a big bummer for everyone.

LYLE. Location, location, location.

MINDY. You let us know if you need help keeping up the sparkle. Mary had a wonderful gift for that.

LYLE. Honey…

MINDY. I can say her name. He's a big boy. Are you a big boy?

KARL. The biggest.

MINDY. I could tell.

(She pins a flier by the front door.)

And spread the word, Karl. Everyone loves seeing their name in peacock feathers!

(She leaves.)

LYLE. You sell peacock feathers?

KARL. No.

LYLE. Fuck. There goes my morning.

(beat)

You wanna get stoned?

KARL. No.

LYLE. You got the perfect alley.

KARL. Help yourself.

*(**LYLE** doesn't.)*

You guys make a living with that racket?

LYLE. It goes hot and cold. Valentine's Weekend we can clear 10K if we space the jobs right. And June's a big month for proposals. Mindy throws a paper route, I do handyman, kayak tours, surfing lessons – whatever covers the nut. How about you?

KARL. Mary kept the books, I never even looked at them, that was part of the agreement.

LYLE. But what do you *do*? I've never seen you before.

KARL. I consult. I've got a little cottage with a big dish and a separate generator and teleconferencing and I wire up and kibitz.

LYLE. So you nailed it. How to live in paradise, make ends meet.

KARL. That was Mary's dream. I was pretty fine with gridlock and good coffee and the phlegmy old bagel guy and a swatch of grass about the size of a magazine.

LYLE. This is better, dude.

KARL. Well you can polish that argument.

(He picks up one of MINDY*'s scones.)*

LYLE. Mindy wants to be partners.

KARL. With me?

LYLE. You've got the primo space.

KARL. She didn't say anything.

LYLE. It's all I've been hearing about. She's scared we'd get tight and gang up on her. Still, she's working up her nerve. This whole courtesy call, that was Mindy checking you out.

*(*KARL *takes a bite of the scone. He chews and chews but it's like sawdust, he can't quite swallow.)*

I should have warned you.

*(*KARL *nods helplessly.)*

Hock it anywhere, I won't tell.

*(*KARL *looks around wildly. No obvious trash can, nothing. He opens a drawer behind the counter, spits the scone into it, quickly closes it.)*

KARL. What's with no gluten?

LYLE. She's not a happy woman. Unsettled. On edge a lot. She's done a systematic elimination of everything that might have a negative impact. She's thinking gluten. I'm thinking me.

KARL. Now there's an icky subtext.

LYLE. Yeah. Well.

(*pause*)

We had a sunset wedding. Right on the cliffs, three years ago. Most amazing day of my life.

KARL. Right.

LYLE. No, amazing. You have to understand that, don't wave it away.

KARL. I'm not.

LYLE. Right then we decided to stay. Live here. Hang onto the moment.

KARL. How's that working?

LYLE. (*not responding right away*) Sometimes I think a place like this…are you religious?

KARL. I'm an Orthodox Jew.

(**LYLE** *looks at him skeptically.*)

Go on.

LYLE. Sometimes I think this place has spirits or love gods that watch over everything that goes on. And we have to find ways to please them.

KARL. Like peacock feathers in the sand.

LYLE. (*remembering*) Shit.

(*back to the point*)

So you have this great day and you think you can have it over and over. When really, everyone gets like two and a half perfect love days a year. And the rest of the time you're hanging out.

KARL. You got a little greedy.

LYLE. Maybe. Sometimes I think the love gods are laughing.

(*pause*)

I sound like an idiot.

KARL. No.

LYLE. Yeah I do.

KARL. No, I've heard them.

(pause)

I remember coming through that door. Just a good guy trying really hard to give my wife the little town dream. Because if I did that…I don't know. We'd be golden. Beyond bad luck. And I walked in and she was glowing, man – the way I *lived* to make her glow, the reason I moved here, bought the store, bought the whole fantasy. So she would glow – *just like that.* Right there in the back room. Making out with Wanda, the aromatherapy dyke.

(beat)

And the love gods laughed so hard, the nectar came out their noses.

LYLE. That's what I'm talking about.

KARL. Everybody who comes in here thinks if they just buy the right thing…

LYLE. *(pulls out a joint)* You sure you don't wanna spark one?

KARL. Go ahead.

LYLE. If I gotta go Marry Me Mona in the sand, I gotta be feeling it.

KARL. Ramona. Marry Me Ramona.

LYLE. *(laughs)* Dude. You saved my ass.

*(He steps into the alley. Again, **KARL** gazes around the empty shop.)*

KARL. *(quietly)* How does anyone do this?

*(**GAIL** and **LESTER** enter.)*

GAIL. Morning, Karl.

KARL. Hello Gail. Lester.

LESTER. How's the Cozy Corner?

KARL. More dozy than cozy. It's a Thursday, I guess.

GAIL. You'd get a lot more people if you washed these windows.

KARL. I keep waiting for that slumlord of mine to send someone around.

LESTER. Ha.

(One look from **GAIL**, *he's done laughing.)*

GAIL. Daily maintenance is every tenant's responsibility.

KARL. Point taken.

GAIL. Your lease agreement details my reasonable expectations.

KARL. I was particularly impressed by their reasonableness.

GAIL. Clean entry, windows, sidewalk. Considerate to all neighbors.

KARL. I am considerate. I offer complimentary scones.

(He holds out the plate and **LESTER** *plucks one.)*

(As **GAIL** *and* **KARL** *talk,* **LESTER** *takes an enthusiastic bite of scone.)*

GAIL. Mary was a particularly good tenant.

KARL. Yes, we're all very proud of her.

*(***GAIL** *notes the sarcasm. She gives him an appraising glance.)*

GAIL. You're not the first person to go through this, Karl. I've had a marriage fall apart. More than once.

*(***KARL** *says nothing.)*

Everything on the inside is screaming run away, clean slate, turn those lemons into lemonade. Everything on the outside is keeping you right where you can't stand to be. Filing papers. Throwing things in boxes. Wrapping up the loose ends.

(softly)

No one's making you stay. If you don't want to.

KARL. I haven't thought that far.

GAIL. Well think now. How do we turn your lemons into lemonade?

*(***KARL**'s *not eager to play.)*

Here's my first thought. One of those mad thoughts, and maybe it leads somewhere.

(**LESTER** *has been chewing furiously, to no avail. He's starting to panic.*)

My friends Doris and Henry. Doris spent the last three years getting their house ready on Meadow Hill, totally redoing it – just a major project in beautiful Mediterranean terra cotta and azure. Tiles that were handcrafted, then hand-broken for an entryway mosaic that, well, you've never seen anything like it. With little olive trees that absolutely thrive in this climate. You liked it, didn't you sweetheart?

(*They both realize* **LESTER***'s in trouble.* **KARL** *quickly throws open the counter drawer.*)

KARL. Right in here, babe.

(**LESTER** *discretely spits out the bit of masticated scone and closes the desk.* **KARL** *hands him some water.*)

You okay?

(**LESTER** *nods, still coming down from his scare.*)

Sorry. With every near-death experience you get a free T-shirt.

GAIL. (*suddenly*) Is someone smoking marijuana?

KARL. We're burning sage.

GAIL. That's not sage.

KARL. It is sage. El Paso sage. Very hard to get. Isn't that what people do around here? Smudge and flush and feng shui some place and then flip it to a wide-eyed yuppie trying to start a new life.

GAIL. Are you mocking me?

KARL. I just saved your husband's life.

GAIL. Let me finish my story. Because Henry finally shows up. For months he's been wrapping up their affairs back in L.A., and he comes up to Sea Spray and he sees

GAIL. *(cont.)* the terra cotta/azure house and he thinks she should have used more of a navy blue. And that was that. Doris asked for the name of my lawyer, and Warren Lane doesn't screw around. Two shakes later, and she's got *a lot* of time on her hands and more spousal support than she knows what to do with. And frankly, this is the sort of thing that would be right up her alley.

(**LYLE** *quietly slips back in from the alley.*)

You've got nine months left on the lease. Here's two easy possibilities. I can rip it up tomorrow, help you sell the inventory. Quick cash and OUT. Or Doris comes in, falls in love like I think she will, you sell her the business AS IS - the lease, the signs, the cobwebs, and everything. You could be on your way next week.

KARL. *(sitting behind the counter)* I don't know.

GAIL. You don't have to know.

(gently)

You're hurt and you're angry. We all understand that. Take some time for *yourself.* Hanging around and moping…that could be embarrassing.

KARL. *(to* **LESTER***)* Are you embarrassed?

LESTER. It's – it's not right.

KARL. *(turning to* **LYLE***)* Are you embarrassed?

LYLE. No, man. Everything is saged and ready for the next blessed phase of your ascension.

GAIL. *(to* **LYLE***)* You're not fooling anybody.

(to **KARL***)*

Would you like to meet Doris?

KARL. Not today.

GAIL. When would be good?

KARL. I don't know Gail. I'll just sit here for awhile until I'm ready.

GAIL. Let's say Sunday.

(to **LYLE***)*

Maybe you can help with the windows.

*(She and **LESTER** leave.)*

*(A moment later **LESTER** slips back in, a little grin on his face. He dips into a display box near the counter.)*

LESTER. Let me have three. She loves moonstones!

*(He leaves a twenty on the counter and darts back out. **KARL** looks over at **LYLE**.)*

KARL. Can you hear it?

LYLE. What?

KARL. *(glances up)* They never stop laughing.

(The lights fade.)

Scene Two

(Lights up. A week has passed and the Cozy Corner hasn't been cleaned once. Empty pizza boxes and magazines and soda cups share some of the shelf space.)

*(**KARL** enters, carrying a bag. He drops his keys, and moves to the T-shirt rack. He pulls **Lucky in Love** off the hanger and drops it in the trash.)*

*(He reaches into his bag and pulls out a hand-lettered shirt that he has made himself. He puts it on the hanger. It reads **My Wife Had an Affair**. He admires it for a moment, then flips it. On the back it says: **And All I Got Was This Lousy T-Shirt**.)*

*(**KARL** wants to display it. He moves to stage left where a few towels decorated with marine life are pinned across the gap between two shelves. He pulls them down, revealing **LYLE** sound asleep on the floor.)*

KARL. *(starting)* Jesus.

LYLE. What?

KARL. How'd you get in here?

LYLE. I'm sorry, man. It was the only place I could think of.

KARL. For what?

LYLE. To hide. I'm in trouble.

KARL. With the law?

LYLE. I don't think so.

> *(beat)*

> Do you have coffee?

KARL. I was gonna run over to Laura's.

LYLE. Would you bring a marked man an extra large?

KARL. I get to hear the story?

LYLE. I can do that.

KARL. You'll watch the store?

LYLE. I can do that too.

KARL. Cream? Sugar?

LYLE. A little whitener. Thanks.

(**KARL** *goes out. After a moment,* **LYLE** *gets up and staggers into the alley.*)

(**MINDY** *enters, carrying another paper plate of fresh baked goods. She puts it on* **KARL**'*s desk and looks around, fretful, frazzled. She sees no sign of* **KARL**, *and cannot help herself. She starts gathering up empty pizza boxes and soda cups. Both arms full of trash, she makes for the back door.*)

LYLE. *(offstage)* Morning, sunshine.

MINDY. *(offstage)* First thing in the morning!?

(*As they argue, a married couple in their 30s enter the store.*)

LYLE. *(offstage)* I don't every day. It's a mood enhancer.

MINDY. *(offstage)* It's a sick habit. A crutch.

LYLE. *(offstage)* I needed a little something before I came over and told you about screwing up.

MINDY. *(offstage)* You don't have to tell me. That poor boy paged me at two in the morning.

LYLE. *(offstage)* He paged me too.

MINDY. *(offstage)* He should have punched you. He should have stabbed you then shot you then run you over, because you are the most stupid selfish childmanfuckup to ever take a breath!!

(*She walks back in while finishing the line and sees the shocked couple.*)

(*pause*)

(**MINDY** *shifts gears, giving the* **HUSBAND** *a big, solicitous smile.*)

MINDY. Are you looking for something special for your sweetie?

HUSBAND. Uh, maybe.

MINDY. You know, moonstones are one of our local treasures. They're a form of feldspar, part of the earth's crust. The Romans said they were formed from drops of moonlight.

WIFE. That's very interesting.

MINDY. I'm just watching the store for a good friend. That's what we do around here, it's like an old-fashioned village. If you're ever interested in a kayak tour or a wild flower walk or –

(twinkling)

– a very perfect proposal, I'm right across the street. The little red sign. Heart Dances. "Your vision, our precision."

HUSBAND. Thank you.

MINDY. *(they're leaving)* You have a lovely day. A perfect day. Everywhere you look, there's a little…

*(She trails off, seeing **KARL**'s new T-shirt on display. The couple is gone, and **LYLE** has appeared in the back door.)*

Is this a joke?

LYLE. I don't think so.

MINDY. "My Wife Had an Affair and All I Got Was this Lousy T-Shirt?!"

(grabbing it)

It's sick. It's a cry for help.

LYLE. You can't take it down.

MINDY. He doesn't know what he's doing.

LYLE. You can't mess with his shop!

MINDY. You were.

LYLE. I was using the alley. I slept here.

MINDY. Why?

(He shrugs.)

Why?

LYLE. I didn't deserve to come home.

*(**KARL** walks in with two cups of coffee.)*

KARL. Morning, Mindy.

*(He hands a cup to **LYLE**.)*

LYLE. You are a golden god.

MINDY. *(holding up shirt)* Is this a joke?

KARL. No. That's a set-up. The joke is on the back.

MINDY. *(tossing it to him)* It's very bad taste.

KARL. Why? Are you cheating on Lyle?

MINDY. This is Sea Spray!

*(She watches **KARL** hanging the shirt back up. She's become righteously incensed.)*

This is a place people go for…The Special. When their feelings are pure and exciting but they need a place that reflects and honors all – all the magic and – and puppy love and…quick pulses and little kisses and…

*(**KARL** pulls another homemade shirt out of the bag, which he holds up for **LYLE** and **MINDY**'s approval. It reads **Just Married** on the front and **Just Shoot Me** on the back.)*

STOP IT! STOP IT!

LYLE. Mindy.

MINDY. You are a sick man. A mean man.

*(**GAIL** and **LESTER** enter the shop.)*

*(**MINDY** is practically in tears)*

He has no right.

*(She storms out. **GAIL** looks at **KARL** stonily.)*

KARL. That actually had very little to do with me.

*(turns to **LYLE**)*

Feel free to back me up.

LYLE. Very little.

GAIL. Not even my first complaint of the day.

KARL. Evelyn called?

GAIL. Of course she did.

KARL. Look, I don't blame her for yelling like that. But off the record, isn't it time we had a moratorium on cranky old babes selling yarn balls?

GAIL. She says you were smashing things in the alley.

KARL. I was. I got this shipment of porcelain otters. And I was thinking – you can't throw a rock in this town without hitting a porcelain otter. So that's what I started doing, I started throwing rocks, which actually felt pretty good for a while. And then I glued them together. And now look.

(He holds up a misshapen porcelain otter with two heads and five arms.)

Only 8.99.

LESTER. That's not right.

KARL. Everyone's a critic.

*(**GAIL** tries to cut through the flippancy.)*

GAIL. Karl, there's a simple way I judge the relationships I have with the tenants in this building. Three questions I ask: Are they good for me? Are they good for the space? Are they good for the town? Good for me is – Do I get my rent on time? Is the tenant considerate and pleasant to deal with? Good for the space is a question of harmony – do the businesses work together? It's also practical: Does it add value? Lester bought me this property five years ago and it's up 6, 7 times in original value. Isn't that right, sweetie?

*(**LESTER** gives her a thumbs-up.)*

Good for the town is trickier. How do you mesh? Are you redundant? Do you complement the experience?

*(He pulls another shirt out of the bag that says **Eunuch**.)*

You think that's funny?

KARL. I think it's bitter. That's as far as I've gotten.

GAIL. Doris keeps asking what's going on with the shop.

KARL. Tell her I've got new inventory.

GAIL. She means how long do I let you throw tantrums in my building?

*(**KARL** stops and faces her.)*

I don't think much longer.

(The two of them have a brief stare-down.)

KARL. Number one: I *am* good for you. I pay my rent, my checks clear. I'm an object of some fascination – or do you visit all your tenants four times a week? Number two: I'm good for the space – I use the alley, which adds value because now it's a "workspace," and you can raise the rent accordingly and by the way that's good for your pocketbook so add that to number one. And as far as Good For the Town – what the fuck, Gail? Are YOU good for the town? You suck out your piece, did you ever donate a park bench or a bit of green space? Did you even vote for the school bond – did Mr. Deep Pockets?

LESTER. That was a poorly written proposal.

KARL. *(counting on his fingers)* Pledge money. Borrow money. Build school. Pay money. And that's poorly written how?

LESTER. It didn't fly for me.

GAIL. You're off the subject.

KARL. The next time you're "Good for the Town" you get three people to sign a letter saying, "Holy shit, she really is good for the town," and I will liquidate and leave on the spot. Until then, don't bully me. Don't ask me, don't offer me, don't Doris me, and keep your FUCKING HANDS OFF MY LEMONS.

GAIL. What?

KARL. Don't count my lemons, talk about lemons, give me lemon recipes. I don't want lemonade.

GAIL. You want me to evict you?

KARL. No. I don't WANT anything. You do whatever you feel like.

GAIL. You're just acting out.

KARL. I was a good guy husband, and I got screwed. The next time I change my life, no one talks me into it.

LYLE. This is so cool. Like an old cowboy code.

GAIL. Shut up, Lyle.

(to **LESTER***)*

Are we all done?

LESTER. *(thrown by the question)* I – I don't…we…

(**KARL** *mischievously holds out the new plate of baked goods.*)

No!

KARL. You need to get back on that horse, buddy.

GAIL. We're all done.

LESTER. Adios, fellas.

(**LESTER** *leaves ahead of her.* **GAIL** *stops in the doorway, turns back to* **KARL.**)

GAIL. I'm not a bitch.

KARL. I never said.

GAIL. *(looks from* **KARL** *to* **LYLE***)* I don't like it. Whatever this is.

(She leaves.)

LYLE. She thinks we're gay.

KARL. It crossed my mind. Now.

(sitting down)

I have waited a long time to hear this.

LYLE. *(lets out a sigh)* I had this big deal to set up. Midnight moonlight proposal. Mindy's all torqued because I keep getting the names wrong: Frank & Coretta. Frank & Coretta. Get the flowers and the champagne and the chocolates in a big ass basket out on Otter Point for FRANK & CORETTA. So I get out there, I set it up perfect, I go down to the beach and the beach is mobbed. The grunion were running last night. You ever do the grunion run?

(**KARL** *shakes his head.*)

They're little stupid fish. You can't use nets. You can't use poles. You gotta catch them with your bare hands, they're coming in on the low tide to mate. Lay their eggs, fertilize their eggs, get the hell out. So they're screwing and spawning and we're grabbing and splashing, everybody gets all sexed up. And the fog rolls in and nobody can see, and it just turns into this wet bump and grind and next thing I know I'm kissing somebody. I'm making out with this sweet-smelling silhouette.

(LYLE pauses.)

KARL. So what happened?

LYLE. You know what happened? My dick woke up. My dick has been numb for eight months, I get into bed with Mindy my eyes are shut I'm spinning the wheel of women. Someone from the past, some chunky butt sitting on my lap in college – anything to get it going. And suddenly I'm on the freezing flipping beach at midnight and my dick is beating on the gates. *I'm alive! I'M ALIVE IN HERE!*

(pause)

It was other women, Karl. That's an asshole thing to say – that's like not the conclusion we're EVER supposed to have. But Jesus Christ, Karl. Other women. That's what I've been missing.

KARL. Wow.

LYLE. *(agreeing)* Wow.

KARL. Did she have a name?

LYLE. Coretta.

(KARL looks at him with complete understanding.)

I'm all messed up here. Can I stay with you?

KARL. Absolutely.

LYLE. At the cottage?

KARL. Oh no.

(He takes a souvenir pillow off the shelf and lays it on the floor where LYLE slept.)

The men of Sea Spray crash right here.

(Lights fade out.)

ACT TWO

(Lights up on The Cozy Corner, four months later. From a presentation standpoint, nothing's new: **KARL** *still can't be bothered to put things in order.)*

(But one thing has changed in a big way: the inventory is completely different, the souvenirs and clothing mainly about bad love and bitterness. It looks like all the anger and disappointment has been flowing out of **KARL**, *right into the store. T-shirts and towels with slogans like:* **I ♥ Heartbreak, Dumped in Sea Spray, On the Rebound** *and – if possible – shirts with a professionally made logo that features a big red heart with a black eye and a lit cigarette.)*

(The front door unlocks and **KARL** *enters, followed by* **GINA**, *a goth high school senior in appropriate Vampira attire.)*

GINA. What about chainsaw earrings?

KARL. Pass.

GINA. Axes?

KARL. We're not about violence.

GINA. You're about misogyny.

KARL. *(shakes head)* I am equally annoyed with both genders.

GINA. Mr. Bergen, I really love your store. I would love to help spread the word.

KARL. I don't have a word. I'm a depressed middle-aged man.

GINA. What if I design something?

KARL. Ever had your heart broken?

GINA. *(shakes head knowingly)* Love is a crock.

KARL. No it's not.

GINA. But all this…

KARL. Romance is real. It's like a million dollar house in a gated community. You and I don't get one. But we can go 40, 50 years thinking we're still gonna get that big break. And then one day we wake up.

*(Right on cue, **RUSSELL** emerges from the back room in his boxers and T-shirt, yawning.)*

RUSSELL. Morning.

KARL. You'll have to wash up at the Texaco across the street.

RUSSELL. I'll be out of your way in a sec.

(He disappears into the back again.)

GINA. Who's that?

KARL. Russell. He has the sign shop. He makes all those beautiful, cutesy signs like my Cozy Corner one, the Dandelion House – the man is a genius at capturing sweetness.

GINA. Why'd he sleep here?

KARL. His marriage. He and Lydia were snarling back and forth for a few days straight and then he went into work and painted a rainbow heart in a teacup and then he couldn't go home.

GINA. Why?

KARL. You tell me.

GINA. No million dollar house.

KARL. Only a plain one. And they're just starting to deal with that.

GINA. But…why sleep here?

KARL. Because he can. It's the only safe place for married men bombing out in Love Town.

(He hands her back her box of samples.)

No shotguns, no chainsaws, no dead babies, no nihilism. Are you disappointed?

(She nods.)

Good. Start there. See where you go.

GINA. Thanks. I really love your shop.

KARL. That's not enough, Gina. You have to be a little pissed at my shop, too.

(As **GINA** *leaves,* **MINDY** *passes her coming in the front door.)*

*(***MINDY** *is much less wound up and chirpy. She's been through a rough patch.)*

MINDY. You had quite a crowd yesterday.

KARL. The ruder I got, the more I sold. Suddenly I'm a tourist trap.

MINDY. Good for you.

KARL. Why is that good for me?

(She doesn't respond.)

And why are you smiling all of a sudden?

MINDY. I got one.

KARL. One what?

MINDY. A catering job. Finally!

KARL. I'll be damned.

MINDY. I'm on pins and needles, you have no idea.

KARL. Just double the gluten, you'll be fine.

MINDY. Oh, very funny.

(beat)

Karl, will you please. Please. Be my taster.

KARL. You don't need me.

MINDY. PLEASE. You're the only one I trust.

(This one's hard to admit.)

You're the only one who's nice to me.

(Pause. **KARL** *can't ignore that.)*

KARL. Who's the client?

MINDY. Big groundbreaking party. Cypress Haven.

KARL. The ones building on Otter Point?

MINDY. It's a shame about that. But they've designed these beautiful solar houses, "green castles" they're calling them. And they're pulling out all the stops for the groundbreaking, they're having a Buddhist monk come and bless the site.

KARL. Wow.

MINDY. Do monks eat soft cheese?

KARL. I've never given it much thought.

MINDY. Well, I'll figure something out. Now that I've got my super secret royal taster!

(**RUSSELL** *walks out of the back room, dressed for the day.* **MINDY** *immediately reins in her excitement.*)

See you later.

(*She's gone.*)

RUSSELL. Hey, what do I owe you, man?

KARL. Your money's no good here. Just watch the store, I need coffee.

RUSSELL. Right on.

(**KARL** *ducks out the front door.* **RUSSELL** *takes a seat at the counter and slips on his iPod. He picks up the local free weekly paper, slides his feet up on the counter and becomes happily oblivious to anyone and anything coming through the door.*)

(*In this case, it's* **LESTER.** *The old fellow looks horrible, overwrought. He pulls a handgun out of his jacket and aims it at* **RUSSELL.***)

(**LESTER** *stands there, waiting for the big shock, the pleading, the begging for mercy. But* **RUSSELL** *doesn't notice him.*)

(**LESTER** *clears his throat.* **RUSSELL** *doesn't hear a thing, he's busy singing to himself.*)

(**KARL** *enters.*)

KARL. Lester, what are you doing?

LESTER. I'm shooting the window washer.

KARL. That's not the window washer. That's the sign painter.

LESTER. I forgot my glasses.

KARL. Go get your glasses if you're going to kill somebody.

*(**LESTER** grumbles and leaves. **KARL** slaps **RUSSELL**'s foot.)*

RUSSELL. *(jumps)* Whoa. You scared me.

KARL. You're a free man.

RUSSELL. Right.

(beat)

I think I'll take the kayak out for a while. Clear my head.

KARL. Sounds good.

RUSSELL. Can I use the cot tonight?

*(**KARL** looks at him carefully.)*

KARL. If you have another fight, yes. If Lydia kicks you out, yes. If you're drunk and confused, absolutely. But if you skip in here all wide-eyed and pumped cause you just walked out on your wife and kids and finally feel like your old true self, then you're sleeping under my dumpster. I hope I'm clear.

RUSSELL. Clear.

KARL. Have a nice day, Russell.

RUSSELL. You too.

*(**LESTER** returns, wearing his glasses. **RUSSELL** brushes past, giving him a friendly pat on the back.)*

Hey, how are ya?

*(He's gone. **LESTER** glares at **KARL**.)*

LESTER. Where's the goddamn window washer?

KARL. What'd he do?

LESTER. He was with my wife.

KARL. The new one? The little one?

LESTER. Monique. I came back to the house for sunscreen. They were both on the deck, laughing. Drinking iced tea.

KARL. That sounds like nothing.

LESTER. She touched his arm!

KARL. Still nothing.

LESTER. I saw what I saw.

(growling)

I could use a drink.

KARL. I told Gail I might need a liquor license.

LESTER. *(bitter)* Don't talk about that woman.

KARL. Yes, boss.

(LESTER *tries to remember what he was going to say.)*

LESTER. Goddamnit. Goddamnit to hell.

(pause)

My neck hurts. My knee hurts. My back hurts, my teeth hurt. You know the only time they don't?

KARL. Making love?

LESTER. *(explodes)* It's twice as bad making love!!

(pause)

It goes away when somebody looks at me with that…I don't know. Hunger. Because they want what I've got. My car, my house, they want me to teach them, they want me to hold them, kiss them, write them a check.

(beat)

This little hippie came up to the house the other day. Wanted to get me to donate a million dollars, two million dollars to the Land Trust. Buy back Otter Point. Kept talking about my legacy. Kept talking about a gift for future generations. It was all horseshit. It was just like two people on prom night. He was the boy, I was the girl. He wanted sex. I wanted respect. He walked home all disappointed. I stood on my front porch feeling fresh. Alive. I'd won another day.

(**LESTER** *is worked up, pacing and waving the gun around.*)

I had a little juice left with Monique, a little currency. She *liked* getting earrings and new handbags – she'd doll up so pretty, hanging on my arm. And then that son of a bitch window washer ruined the game.

KARL. You're gonna shoot him for iced tea?

LESTER. Damn right.

KARL. I caught my wife kissing another woman. I didn't shoot anybody.

LESTER. That's because you're a pansy! You shoulda shot them both and burned this place to the ground.

KARL. Give me the gun. Give me –

(**LESTER** *won't.*)

I don't even like you. You're rich and selfish and put up ugly buildings.

LESTER. Screw you.

(**KARL** *grabs for the gun and, in the briefest of struggles, it goes off. A single shot fired. At which point* **KARL** *yanks it away from* **LESTER**, *who immediately looks deflated.*)

(**LESTER** *glances out the window*) Shit.

KARL. What?

LESTER. Don't tell her I did it!

(*He disappears into the back room as…***GAIL** *enters. Looking radiant.*)

GAIL. Was that a gun shot?

KARL. Balloon. I keep over-inflating the Mylar.

GAIL. Ah.

KARL. You're back.

GAIL. Just last night.

KARL. So how was…

GAIL. Costa Rica.

(pause, as she notices)

That's a gun right there.

KARL. Yes. Bit of a coincidence.

GAIL. Lester had one just like it. Made me hold it once in bed, right up to his head.

KARL. *(very loud, overlapping)* Wow, so Costa Rica! Tell me everything.

GAIL. It was fab-u-loussss. My son from my first marriage was halfway through construction on his house. And the locals were just ripping him off, seven ways from Sunday. I went down there and got the whole project on track – under budget, only ten days late – that's to be expected, they can't go the bathroom without having some kind of festival. I even found this beautiful glaze to treat the bricks, it gave them a golden sheen. The whole place is like an Inca palace.

KARL. And now you're back for the holidays.

GAIL. They didn't want me around.

KARL. Your son?

GAIL. His wife, really. She's a lovely girl. She just needs to get her way, whether it's the informed choice or not.

KARL. Well. It's nice to see you.

(beat)

I assume you're here to throw me out.

GAIL. Not at all. Apparently you're doing well.

KARL. That's a vicious rumor.

GAIL. Two write-ups in the local paper, lots of word of mouth. Someone wants to license the shirts?

KARL. "Bitterware." I'm embarrassed to even say it.

GAIL. I was wrong about you.

KARL. Is that some kind of apology?

GAIL. No. That's me reconsidering certain landlord rules.

KARL. Like what?

GAIL. Never ask out a tenant.

KARL. *(under his breath)* Not right now.

GAIL. Shhh. I'm just inviting you to dinner.

(coy, softly)

Is that really so shocking?

KARL. No, I –

GAIL. We can talk about the lease.

KARL. I guess it's time.

GAIL. Have a nice bottle of wine.

KARL. Yeah. Um.

GAIL. I've never flustered you before, Karl. It's kind of sweet.

(quietly)

I'm onto you.

KARL. How so?

GAIL. Mr. Bitterware is a big softy.

*(She's moved in close, ready for a kiss if **KARL** is. But he's acutely aware of **LESTER** in the next room.)*

KARL. Let's do this later.

GAIL. You think I'm old.

KARL. No, no I –

GAIL. I'll do things you're scared to think about. Ask Lester.

KARL. I'd rather keep him out of it.

GAIL. *(laughs)* He was out of it even when he was in.

*(This is killing **KARL**. At that moment, **LYLE** comes striding through the door.)*

LYLE. GREAT GODDAMN DAY TO BE A WINDOW WASHER!

*(**KARL** buries his head; a man trapped in the eye of a shitstorm.)*

GAIL. All right, Bitterboy. I know where to find you.

*(She leaves with a smile. **LYLE** continues his jubilant booming.)*

LYLE. Seriously, I pity every man who doesn't wash windows for a living!!

KARL. You gotta get out of here.

LYLE. *(brandishing his smoke bag)* Not without a victory toke.

KARL. Lyle!

(Too late. He's disappeared into the back room, on his way to the alley. A second later he pops back in.)

LYLE. Why is Lester sleeping on the cot?

*(**KARL** sighs with relief.)*

KARL. He came here to kill you.

LYLE. He should.

*(off **KARL**'s look)*

Dude, she attacked me. The moment she brought out the iced tea, it was clear what she wanted.

(beat)

Don't be judging me.

KARL. I'm not. I'm sitting here thinking I'd have a much better time if I could be a callous shithead like you.

LYLE. They *need* me, Karl! All these divorced and near-divorced women. Married for security – or sticking around for security, whatever, they all resent that they NEED security, so now they have to show the world they can still cut loose. And here comes Lyle the Window Wizard. And I lather up the glass and start making little smiley faces and curvy curves, and ten minutes later I'm running the squeegee over their naked ass and here comes the Spite Sex. The Goddamnit I Still Like Sex sex. And then they write me a check and I go surfing.

(beat)

For the first time in my life, this stupid town makes sense.

(As he heads for the alley, joint in his mouth, the lights fade.)

*(**KARL** remains in place, and after a few seconds the lights come back up.)*

(It's the same day, but now closing time.)

*(**KARL** is totaling up the day's receipts. A bleary **LESTER** comes out the back room. He can't quite believe what his watch is telling him.)*

LESTER. It's not really six.

KARL. Sleep of the Gods, man.

LESTER. I feel a bit…better. He came by, didn't he?

KARL. I saw him.

LESTER. Did he bed her?

KARL. It was pretty much what you expected.

LESTER. She's a dirty little bitch.

KARL. No, she's all shiny now.

LESTER. *(sighs)* Where'm I gonna find another?

KARL. What's your big hurry?

LESTER. What the hell do you think?

*(**KARL** has no adequate response.)*

I never had a three-way.

KARL. Sorry?

LESTER. A ménage a trois. Never had one.

KARL. So?

LESTER. So! I always thought it would happen. A fellow like me, why wouldn't it? Rub a dub dub, everyone in the tub. It sounded so…debonair. Now it's too late. Too late for the rest of my life.

(pause)

How'd you end up so lucky?

KARL. I don't feel lucky.

LESTER. Then pay attention. You even see where the bullet went?

*(He walks over and picks up the **I ♥ Heartbreak** shirt. He shows **KARL** that the heart shape has a hole in it.)*

That's a limited edition right there. I'll take half the profits.

KARL. Deal.

(**MINDY** *enters, sees* **LESTER.**)

MINDY. Oh. I'm sorry, I…

(*holds up a plate of food*)

Calamari croquettes.

(*barely audible*)

Three kinds of dipping sauce.

LESTER. I was just saying goodnight.

(*shoots* **KARL** *a grin*)

Start paying attention.

(*He's gone.* **MINDY** *moves forward.*)

KARL. Smells great.

MINDY. (*almost breathless*) I like it because it's taking something from the sea, something mysterious, the giant squid of course, and then *taming* it and making it wonderful and fluffy and then poof, wasabi mayonnaise.

KARL. If that isn't the perfect metaphor.

MINDY. Don't make fun. Lyle used to say I'm always chasing couplets that won't rhyme.

KARL. That sounds too good for Lyle.

MINDY. He said I was always chasing "flipping rhymes."

KARL. You were the best editor he ever had.

(**MINDY** *chokes up for a moment.*)

Hey, sorry.

MINDY. That was the sort of appreciation…I was never going to get…

(*beat*)

I'm doing fine. Moved on. He's got that Peter Pan thing.

KARL. Not quite Peter. Just a big Lost Boy.

(**MINDY** *laughs.*)

MINDY. Quick. These are getting cold.

(almost mischievous)

Can I give you the blindfold test?

KARL. Why?

MINDY. For fun.

KARL. I can close my eyes.

MINDY. Party-pooper.

KARL. Just go.

*(He waits, eyes closed. **MINDY** dips a croquette, and gently sends it into his mouth.)*

(chewing) Gingery. Very sweet, soy, really going Asian here. Makes it more of a tempura thing. Which is good, I don't know if that's the effect you want. But I like the afterburn, that's great.

(finishes, starts groping)

Water. Must. Clean. Palate.

*(**MINDY**, delighted, hands him some water. He drinks a little, gargles – he's goofing around, playing the part of the connoisseur for hire.)*

Hit me, baby.

*(Again, **MINDY** lovingly places a croquette with sauce in **KARL**'s mouth.)*

(chewing through his commentary) Ah, the wasabi mayo. The fire of the great east tamed by the artery-clogging artistry of the Midwest. A global party in my mouth, and that does not even address how unbelievable these croquettes are.

MINDY. Thank you.

KARL. You have so found your thing. It's a beauty to behold.

*(**MINDY** says nothing, hands him the water.)*

Bring it.

*(**MINDY** hesitates, and then…she dips her finger in the third, red sauce and runs it around her lips.)*

(She bends over…but can't quite muster the nerve.)

*(**KARL** opens his eyes.)*

KARL. *(cont.)* There a problem?

(She nods.)

Cooking problem?

(She shakes her head.)

Is that…cocktail sauce on your lips?

(With a gasp of impatience, fear, desire, she kisses him hard. It lasts a few delirious seconds, and then they come up for air.)

MINDY. No, no. Do this with me.

KARL. Mindy…

MINDY. It's so happy.

KARL. Mindy, no.

MINDY. But you see? Don't you see it?

*(**KARL** doesn't know what to see. Or say.)*

You get left and I get left and we're right across the street.

KARL. Mindy. Hey…

MINDY. These things happen for a reason. That's the miracle.

(pause)

KARL. Here's the miracle. Terrible things happen, and we make up stories about why it's okay. Why it was meant to be. And that's the miracle, Mindy. We have that grace, that beautiful bullshit.

*(**MINDY** starts crying quietly.)*

I'm sorry.

(He gets up, puts his arms around her.)

I'm not your happy ending.

(He stands there, holding her.)

(The door opens and **GAIL** *stands there, dressed for the evening.)*

I'm not anyone's happy ending.

(He continues to hold **MINDY**, *looking right at* **GAIL**. *The lights fade.)*

ACT THREE

(Lights up on The Cozy Corner. Another four months have passed. The general make-up of the store remains the same, with the addition of a few prominent hand-made signs. They read:

Lost Our Lease!

Closing Sale!

Everything 5¢!

Just 2 Days Left

(There is also an elegant urn on the counter, with a silver scoop hanging from a chain.)

*(**GINA**, the goth girl, is behind the counter. The place is crawling with customers – as many as can be managed.)*

(A customer approaches, holding a necklace.)

CUSTOMER. How much is this?

GINA. A nickel.

CUSTOMER. How about the T-shirts?

GINA. A nickel. Everything's a nickel.

CUSTOMER. *(holding up a crab ashtray)* But –

GINA. A nickel.

CUSTOMER. It's chipped on the bottom.

GINA. Three cents.

*(She makes the sale and will continue to conduct trans-actions through her dialogue with **ALEX**, a young man who enters the store. He tries hard to affect an air of cool.)*

ALEX. Karl Bergen around?

GINA. He's sort of in and out today.

ALEX. I called to talk to him. I'm from the paper.

GINA. The Pine Breeze?

ALEX. Right. I'm Alex Dern.

GINA. I know you.

ALEX. Yeah, you look familiar. You still in school?

GINA. Senior year.

ALEX. This a part-time gig?

GINA. Sorta. I keep trying to sell him stuff and he keeps saying no. But he lets me help out.

ALEX. So you're an artist?

GINA. Until proven normal. You're a writer?

ALEX. I don't know what I am. Deferred freshman year. My dad calls me the waffling suckhole.

GINA. You should get that on a business card.

ALEX. Thanks.

> (**KARL** *appears in the doorway to the back room. He eavesdrops on the two of them.*)

So what's the deal? Why are you going out of business?

> (*By way of response,* **GINA** *puts up another handmade sign:* **The Witch Doesn't Get It**.)

The witch being?

GINA. Our landlady.

ALEX. She doesn't get what?

GINA. Whadya got?

ALEX. Not real big on goth girls?

GINA. *(snaps)* I'm not goth anymore. I'm just stuck with these clothes until my sister takes me shopping.

ALEX. Sorry.

GINA. Whatever.

ALEX. It looked like a dress code.

GINA. Look harder.

> (*She flashes him bright purple socks.*)

ALEX. Ooh. Rebel, rebel.

(**GINA** *smiles.*)

Okay, what's it like working for a guy who hates love?

GINA. He doesn't hate love. He hates LOVE-little TM-copyright-an exclusive division of blahdey-blah.

ALEX. What about you?

GINA. He doesn't hate me at all.

ALEX. No. Are you a cynic too?

GINA. *(impatient)* It's not cynical. It's having a code, and loyalty – you know I can see you spying!

(**KARL** *steps forward, a little sheepish.*)

Tell him about Lester.

ALEX. Who's Lester?

KARL. Lester was my friend. Sort of a friend. A cranky pain in the ass. When his fourth or sixth or seventh marriage blew up, he started hanging out here a lot. He liked the place, it amused him. And when he died he left me his ashes. To be sold on the counter, by the register. A buck a scoop.

ALEX. Wow.

(*They both regard the stained glass urn.* **KARL** *props up a little cardboard sign:* **Lester's Ashes $1.00**.)

KARL. Have a little. On the house.

ALEX. Uh…

(**KARL** *dips into the urn and sprinkles some in* **ALEX***'s direction.*)

KARL. Once we started selling these, the shitstorm hit. We were shut down briefly by the health inspector. We had a lot of pissed-off letters in the local paper. The mayor tried to intervene. The Lion's Club threatened to beat me up, but they're all, like, 105 and there wasn't enough extra oxygen. I was decried and derided on the floor of the California State Senate. And ultimately, the landlady pulled our lease.

GINA. She used to be married to Lester.

ALEX. I should be writing this down.

KARL. Probably.

(*handing him an album*)

Here's the scrapbook.

GINA. The life and times of Instant Lester.

KARL. I couldn't see refusing a dead man. Some things are more important than…good manners.

GINA. So she's kicking him out.

ALEX. (*flipping pages*) This is a very cool story.

KARL. Then write a very cool piece.

ALEX. I don't suppose I could borrow this?

KARL. If you bring it back tomorrow.

ALEX. I promise.

KARL. I'm going to be busy. But Gina will help you any way you need.

ALEX. This is perfect.

KARL. Maybe you'd like to have lunch?

ALEX. Lunch will be great.

(*to* **GINA**)

See you tomorrow.

GINA. Apparently.

(*He leaves. She gives* **KARL** *a withering look.*)

Real subtle.

KARL. What?

GINA. The pathetic Mr. Cupid move.

KARL. Ah. You're having one of those teenage paranoid moments.

GINA. Shut up.

KARL. A very nice young man, though. In a scruffy, aimless, bad choice, your-mother-would-hate-him kind of way.

(**LYLE** *blows through the door.*)

LYLE. Dude, it's been ages. Quick catch-up, okay? New lady, new life – epic, epic, very heavy, very powerful. Check this.

(He places a large, pink seashell on the counter.)

KARL. I'm afraid to ask.

LYLE. It's a seashell. Full of aromatherapy powder, granules – I'm sorry, I said *aromatherapy*.

KARL. The wounds have healed.

LYLE. You put the whole thing in the bath. It fizzes up, makes you perky, rejuvenated. It's the cheesiest, sexiest thing I ever bought in my life.

KARL. Sucking up to the Love Gods, are we?

LYLE. Freaking out, man. I'm in love, I'm in fear, I've got nothing solid under my feet.

(almost pleading)

I – I gotta use the alley.

KARL. Anytime.

LYLE. You're a golden god.

(hands him the shell)

Don't sell this, okay?

KARL. Not exactly my style.

*(**LYLE** disappears into the back.)*

*(**KARL** places the big pink shell behind the counter, out of sight.)*

*(**GINA***'s been waiting this whole time to say something.)*

GINA. So…I've got a new one.

KARL. Let's see.

*(She pulls out a necklace with a metallic pendant. **KARL** examines it.)*

Half a heart.

GINA. Right.

KARL. So it matches some other half a heart you give to your *Twoo Wuv?*

GINA. No, it's just half a heart. Period. The end.

(**KARL** *looks at it more carefully and starts to smile.*)

(**GAIL** *enters in a mood.*)

GAIL. Who made the signs?

KARL & GINA. *(at the same time)* I did.

KARL. Okay, she did. What of it?

GAIL. They're personal attacks.

KARL. They're statements of truth.

GAIL. "THE WITCH doesn't GET IT?"

KARL. Which part did you find offensive?

GAIL. Why am I a witch? – I'm just protecting my investment. And obviously I *get it*: some demented dying man tried to top your sick sense of humor.

KARL. He was burned by every woman he married. He thought he could protect the rest of us.

GAIL. That's bullshit.

KARL. A little sprinkle before bedtime, keep the harpies away.

GAIL. We are done with this topic. I'm signing a brand new lease with Doris – finally – and she's thrilled – finally – so we are done with *everything*, Karl. Except the signs.

KARL. I'm sorry, Ms. Lanson put a lot of effort into those.

(**GAIL** *fixes an icy stare on* **GINA.**)

GAIL. Take them down.

KARL. *(under his breath)* She has no power until the day after tomorrow.

GINA. I'd rather not.

GAIL. *(dialing her cell phone)* Fine, I have someone who will.

(*A cell phone starts ringing in the alley.*)

LYLE. *(offstage – answering)* Hey baby! I'm coming – I'm hung up in traffic.

(**GAIL** *marches over to the back room and shouts towards* **LYLE**.)

GAIL. Then get my car out of the alley, dimwit!

(**LYLE** *rushes back in, stubbing out his joint.*).

LYLE. I'm here. I'm sorry. That was just a quickie.

(beat)

What's up?

(**GAIL** *gives him a disapproving look.*)

GAIL. I want every sign about witches and landladies pulled down.

LYLE. Right. I'm on it.

GAIL. *(still annoyed)* Oh, you're "on it." You're sure?

LYLE. I'm sure.

(They're now standing close together. **GAIL** *shifts to a softer tone.)*

GAIL. Sorry I got snippy.

LYLE. Red hot chakras, baby. Don't ever apologize.

(They kiss tenderly and she leaves. **LYLE** *turns to* **KARL***, who's been watching almost open-mouthed.)*

KARL. You're shitting me.

LYLE. She's a great lady, dude. And I'm way more tuned in to the monogamy thing. She lets me paint. She lets me surf. I've got two canvases going in the garage which she's converting into a studio and they're really good, man. I'm definitely getting better. No one else would ever give me that chance.

(off **KARL** *saying nothing)*

So ha ha. I'm a trophy wife.

KARL. Does Mindy know?

LYLE. Mindy disappeared. She, like, hooked up with some methane tycoon.

KARL. So everybody's gold-digging. I never got the memo.

LYLE. Hey, you had your chance. From what I heard.

> (**KARL** *dismisses this with a wave.*)

I think that's why she's booting you.

GINA. That's what I said.

KARL. Nah. She's pissed about the Lester scoop. That crossed some line.

LYLE. She's catching unbelievable flak, dude. From the moment you put your signs up. There's a petition going to keep you around.

GINA. A petition?!

KARL. From who?

LYLE. Evelyn.

KARL. The yarn biddy?

LYLE. And some of the others on Main Street.

KARL. They hate me. They hate the store.

LYLE. Yeah, but they love your customers.

GINA. You can fight this, I know you can.

> (**KARL** *says nothing.*)

LYLE. So where you gonna go?

KARL. Back to beautiful Culver City. Older, wiser, a little less employable.

LYLE. It's been real.

> (*shaking hands*)

Real. Unreal. Surreal. I gotta get those signs and I'll be out of your hair.

KARL. I like the signs, Lyle.

LYLE. Yeah, but. Gail wants them down.

KARL. Too bad.

LYLE. Come on, Karl.

KARL. You want to take those down, you'll have to fight me.

GINA. Karl…

KARL. I've never fought for anything. But I think I'm ready.

(A tense pause – interrupted by **LYLE**'s *cell phone ringing. He glances at it.)*

LYLE. Aw, shit.

(answering)

I'll be right there. RIGHT there.

(He hangs up and looks at **KARL**, *a little desperate.)*

Can we just do this…like adults.

KARL. You first.

*(***LYLE*** has no next move.)*

Gina. Did you ever settle on a price?

LYLE & GINA. What?

KARL. For the art work. I heard 20, then I heard 30.

GINA. I…

KARL. *(to* **LYLE***)* 25 each. You want, she'll sign and number them.

LYLE. I didn't think you were this sleazy.

KARL. I'm not selling my ass for garage space.

*(***LYLE*** *angrily peels off some bills and hands them to* **GINA**.*)*

GINA. Thanks.

*(***LYLE*** *starts to leave.)*

KARL. Don't forget your signs.

LYLE. Fuck off.

(He pulls them down angrily and stomps out. **KARL** *turns to* **GINA**.*)*

KARL. Congratulations. Your first sale.

GINA. Yeah, right.

KARL. Next time, purely on talent. Which reminds me.

(He pulls out her necklace.)

This is perfect.

GINA. You mean it?

KARL. I do. Can I buy it?

GINA. You can have it.

KARL. No, I'm buying it. Go make more, as many as you can, we'll sell them 15 a pop – we've still got one more day. Go get some signs printed: two free T-shirts – two free ANY of my crap – with every necklace.

GINA. You're kidding.

KARL. This is the best thing I ever got to sell.

GINA. You can fight her, Karl. My uncle's a lawyer, he'll look at the lease, he says –

KARL. *(won't hear of it)* This is what I get. This is how it goes down. Gail's a witch, I'm a martyr. And somewhere, Lester is laughing his head off.

(He tosses her a key.)

I need you to open up tomorrow. I'm going to be a little late. Go get those signs ready, okay?

*(She's gone. **KARL** takes a moment, then launches into high gear. He puts up the **Closed** sign, pulls out a backpack from under the desk and starts filling it with cash, documents, letters, whatever he thinks he needs. He's getting ready to slip away.)*

*(As he does this, an elegant-looking woman appears in the doorway. We might not recognize **MINDY** at first.)*

MINDY. So it's true.

KARL. Mindy…

MINDY. You're shutting down.

KARL. Yeah. Sorta painted myself in a corner.

(beat)

You look great.

MINDY. Thanks.

KARL. So who is he? Mr. Right.

MINDY. His name is Tom. Thomas. He…well, he makes money. I mean, it's dull. He buys and sells small to medium methane manufacturing –

KARL. Okay, I get it.

MINDY. He was at the groundbreaking. He loved the croquettes.

KARL. I'll be damned.

MINDY. He bought one of the Otter Point lots. I couldn't
believe it, it's probably my favorite sunset proposal spot.

KARL. Is that where he asked you?

MINDY. He asked me in Cleveland.

KARL. Also very lovely.

MINDY. It's all lovely. We travel. I cook like crazy. Those
catering jobs gave me so much anxiety, but I cook for
Tom and his clients and friends – we must do a big
dinner every week. It's so much fun.

KARL. Mindy. I'm really happy for you.

MINDY. Why would you say that? You of all people.

KARL. I –

MINDY. *(angry)* Why didn't you leave? Why did you stick
around and make fun?

KARL. *(quietly)* That was never the point. I tried to make
someone happy – we know how that went. And after,
I just wanted to be left alone. So I could watch Mary's
little dream shop crash and burn and shrivel and I
could sit in the wreckage until I finally felt like getting
up and walking away.

(beat)

And I guess that's today.

(beat)

You do have a really lovely glow.

MINDY. Anti-depressants. Duh.

KARL. Well, tip your doctor.

(He packs up the last of his stuff.)

MINDY. *(near tears)* He's smug. He drinks too much. He
makes puns. We're eating ourselves to death. Sometimes when he touches me I...I want to shed my skin.

(pause)

KARL. Then this is for you.

*(**KARL** hands her **GINA**'s necklace.)*

Nobody has the other half. Okay?

(He speaks gently, but with true urgency.)

Don't do it. Don't marry him for money, don't marry for panic, or the lot line or the kitchen island – don't marry him. Don't. Don't fucking marry him. Just sit with it.

MINDY. *(almost a whisper)* Who sits with me?

*(Before **KARL** can respond, **GAIL** and **LYLE** re-enter. **GAIL** is livid.)*

GAIL. You've got some nerve. What you did to Lyle.

LYLE. *(noticing **MINDY**, quietly to **GAIL**)* Can we not do this?

GAIL. Do you think it's clever or – or macho, making him *buy* the signs? Just because it's *my* money?!

KARL. Common decency –

GAIL. You have NO COMMON DECENCY, or you wouldn't shake him down like – like the neighborhood bully!!

KARL. Common decency requires I point out you're neutering your boyfriend in front of his ex-wife.

GAIL. Shut up, Karl.

KARL. Sorry, Mom.

*(to a miserable **LYLE**)*

The cot is open. Last night ever.

MINDY. I should get going.

*(But **GINA** comes in the door, carrying new signs.)*

GAIL. Give me the money. Right now.

GINA. It wasn't my idea.

GAIL. Just give it to me.

GINA. I already spent ten on signs, he told me to.

GAIL. GIVE ME THE SIGNS!

GINA. They're not about you!

GAIL. *(grabbing for them)* Bullshit!

GINA. Let go!

GAIL. *(She's got* **GINA** *by the wrist, but can't reach the signs.)* LYLE!

MINDY. *(stepping in front of* **LYLE***)* Don't you dare.

(It's about to be a free-for all. **GINA** *and* **GAIL** *struggling,* **MINDY** *and* **LYLE** *squaring off…)*

*(***KARL** *picks up the urn of ashes. No one is watching as he hurls it to the floor behind the counter. Everyone freezes at the CRASH!)*

KARL. Oh my god. NOBODY MOVE!

*(***KARL** *grabs a dustpan and a whisk broom from the wall and slips around the counter.)*

Lester! I am such a klutz. I am so sorry!

(He disappears from view behind the counter, muttering and cursing himself while he cleans up.)

Ugh, what a mess.

*(***GAIL** *turns to* **GINA***, still a little out of breath.)*

GAIL. Let me tell you something. And you can tell all your little friends at high school or wherever you're flunking that you heard this from The Witch, the real live witch: Nobody *gives* you anything. And when you get old, they give you even less. And you will not, for a moment, make me ashamed about wanting my fair share of fun and – and pleasure and money. And men. And wine. And if that happens to be what *you* want too, only I'm 40 years older and have so much more and it doesn't seem fair – and will there be any left for you and how can you make sure? I mean, if that's what's bothering you…don't sit around here helping Karl mock me. Be better than that. Try and learn something, for god's sake.

KARL. *(out of sight, from behind the counter)* I have a question for the mistress of darkness.

(He rises up, dustpan in his hand.)

What would happen if I dump this in the trash?

(**GAIL** *doesn't respond.*)

KARL. *(cont.)* Take it out later, maybe scatter around the beach.

(*beat*)

What happens?

GAIL. You're serious?

KARL. What happens?

GAIL. *(considers this)* You can have another year.

(*pause*)

(**KARL** *slams the whole dustpan into the trash with a flourish.*)

(*The tension dissipates instantly.*)

LYLE. That was epic. I mean, that was –

KARL. If you people don't mind. We're closed for business.

(**MINDY** *looks at him with a tentative smile.*)

MINDY. I'll see you...

KARL. Tomorrow. That would be tomorrow.

MINDY. Okay.

(*She leaves.* **GAIL** *goes up to* **KARL.**)

GAIL. I was starting to worry. Doris can be a real bore.

(*She gives him a smile of détente, and heads for the door.*)

KARL. Hey!

(**GAIL** *turns.*)

Short-term memory is not your boyfriend's strong suit. He wanted to give you this.

(**KARL** *reaches under the counter and brings up the large pink seashell.*)

GAIL. What is it?

LYLE. It's a bath shell. Filled with salts, powders – aroma-therapy.

KARL. He likes you, Gail. Against all odds.

GAIL. *(almost flustered)* You are such a sweet...

LYLE. Want to give it a whirl?

GAIL. Oh! The perfect end to a grueling day.

*(They leave, arm in arm, **GAIL** carrying the shell.)*

GINA. Gag-o-fucking-rama.

KARL. *(quietly)* As it turns out, I don't need you to open up tomorrow.

*(**GINA** rounds on him angrily.)*

GINA. Who ARE YOU?!

KARL. Who do you think?

GINA. I don't know anymore. You gave up, you caved – how could you fold like that? – no fight, no code, just some big runny, kiss-ass – WHY DID YOU DO THAT?

KARL. *(softly)* I was leaving too soon.

(beat)

I didn't know how to stop it.

GINA. So you dumped Lester? Flushed him away!

KARL. *(gathering his things)* Maybe he'll forgive me.

GINA. I wouldn't! Not when you go for the cheap glory grab.

(mocking)

Oh, King Karl. Oh, you make everyone so happy!

KARL. *(with wonder)* I know. This could be bad for business.

(pausing at the door)

I wouldn't worry about Lester. I think he's still laughing.

GINA. Why would he be?!

KARL. He's about to take a bath with Lyle and Gail.

*(**KARL** shuts the door as the lights black out.)*

PROPERTIES, COSTUMES AND SETS

The entire play takes place in a beach town tourist trap souvenir shop that gradually transforms into one man's bitter parody of a beach town souvenir shop.

ACT 1, SCENE 1 establishes Mary's Cozy Corner, which should be dressed with curios and knickknacks that reflect romance by the sea. Fuzzy stuffed seals, shells glued into heart shapes, and T-shirts with slogans like **I ♥ Sea Spray**, **Lucky in Love** and **Just Engaged**. Props specific to the action are:

> A paper plate with inedible scones
> A joint
> A box with shiny moonstones

ACT 1, SCENE 2 props:
> Empty pizza boxes and fast food trash
> A T-shirt that says **My Wife Had an Affair** on the front, with **And All I Got Was This Lousy T-Shirt** on the back
> A T-shirt that says **Just Married** on the front and **Just Shoot Me** on the back
> A T-shirt that says **Eunuch**
> Another paper plate of baked treats
> Two cups of coffee to go
> A broken and re-glued porcelain otter with 2 heads and 5 arms

ACT 2 props:
> T-shirts and towels with slogans like: **I ♥ Heartbreak, Dumped in Sea Spray, On the Rebound**. (Note: The **I ♥ Heartbreak** shirt must have a bullet hole through the heart.)
> T-shirts with a professionally made logo that features a big red heart with a black eye and a lit cigarette
> An iPod
> A gun that fires
> A plate of appetizers and dipping sauces

ACT 3 props:
> Hand written signs that read *Lost Our Lease! Closing Sale! Everything 5¢! Just 2 Days Left* and *The Witch Doesn't Get It*
> Various souvenirs, including a necklace and a crab ashtray
> A stained glass urn with ashes and a cardboard sign: "Lester's Ashes $1.00"
> A large pink seashell filled with bath powder
> A cell phone that rings on cue
> A necklace with half a metallic heart
> A backpack
> A dustpan and whisk broom
> A stack of new signs

OTHER TITLES AVAILABLE FROM SAMUEL FRENCH

THE SECRET LIFE OF SEAGULLS

Henry Meyerson

Dramatic Comedy / 2m, 2f, Doubling Possible

Anne and Don, married ten years, are on vacation in Florida. Anne is inanely chattering on about beaches, seagulls and garbage dumps. Don, fed up with Anne's incessant chatter, walks away leaving Anne, much to her surprise, sitting on the beach alone. Don has gone to visit his friend Jim, a man of little insight but great obsession about golf, to tell him that he has left Anne. Jim, in turn, has just returned from a golfing vacation to discover his wife, Sandy, has apparently left him. George, a seagull who lives a contented life with his wife, Ethel, on the Staten Island landfill, has just arrived on the Florida beach and meets Fred, a seagull without ties but with a dark past.

The Secret Live of Seagulls follows these four humans and Fred as they attempt to define themselves, their lives, relationships and values. George, the Staten Island seagull, however, is quite content being who he is.

www.ingramcontent.com/pod-product-compliance
Lightning Source LLC
Chambersburg PA
CBHW070417120726
47909CB00005B/1688